THE LITTLE BOY STAR

A publication of
Milk & Cookies Press, a division of ibooks, inc.

Distributed by Publishers Group West
1700 Fourth Street, Berkeley, CA 94710

ibooks, inc.
24 West 25th Street, 11th floor, New York, NY 10010

ISBN: 1-59687-172-5
First ibooks, inc. printing: April 2006
10 9 8 7 6 5 4 3 2 1

Editor - Dinah Dunn
Associate Editor - Robin Bader

Designed by Edie Weinberg

Library of Congress Cataloging-in-Publication Data available

Manufactured in China

THE LITTLE BOY STAR

BY RACHEL HAUSFATER

ILLUSTRATED BY OLIVIER LATYK

WITH AN INTRODUCTION BY
DAVID A. ADLER

TRANSLATION BY JOËLLE ZIMMERMAN

MILK &
COOKIES
PRESS ™

DISTRIBUTED BY PUBLISHERS GROUP WEST

In the years following the first World War,
Germany was in trouble. In the early 1920s its
money was almost worthless. By the 1930s,
millions of people had lost their jobs. Many were
hungry and homeless.

Throughout that time, Nazi party leader
Adolf Hitler campaigned for power. He spoke on
street corners and in beer halls. He shouted,
waved his fists, and blamed the Jews and others
for all his nation's troubles. His shouts were
heard. In the July and November 1932 elections,
his Nazi party received more votes than any
other party. By January 1933, Hitler was made
the nation's chancellor.

Hitler's hate-filled ideas and the violence
he incited in his followers quickly changed the
country. In the coming months and years,
horrible concentration camps were opened. These
were prisons for people the Nazis called "enemies
of the state." Books were burned. Jews and others
were thrown out of their jobs, homes, and many
were attacked. Children were thrown out of schools.

In March 1938, the Germans took over Austria, a neighboring country. Beginning in September 1939, they attacked Poland and then other countries in Europe. Nazis brought their hatred to each country their army conquered. World War II spread across Europe.

In many places, Nazis made Jews wear six-pointed stars on their clothes so they would be easy to identify. Jews were forced onto trains and taken to concentration camps, which were now death camps. By 1945, in what was later called the Holocaust, some six million Jews and millions of other innocent people had been murdered. Those who survived had to somehow rebuild their lives, often without the families, friends, and people they loved.

—David A. Adler,
author of THE NUMBER ON MY GRANDFATHER'S ARM, CHILD OF THE WARSAW GHETTO, and the CAM JANSEN mysteries.

He was a little
boy who did not know
he was a star.

But that's what he was told.

At first, he was
happy, he was proud.
He thought it was
nice to be a star.

But this star
had too many points.

So the little
Boy Star started
to feel ashamed.

And the more ashamed
he felt, the bigger the
star grew.

After a while,
you could no longer
see the little boy
at all.

All you could see
was the star.

Around him,
the other stars
were running in all
directions in a panic...

because the star hunters
were getting
nearer.

One day, the hunters
caught the stars
and took them away
in dark trains.

And the little Boy Star saw
the big Daddy Stars,
the gentle Mommy Stars and all
the Baby Stars go into the night.

And then were no more.

The little Boy Star
crossed his arms
and tried to smother
all the light
he had in him.
He pretended
he was no longer a star.

And it made him feel
as if he was no longer
a little boy.

He stayed hidden
for a long time.

It was dark
outside and inside.

Finally the night
ended
and the little boy
was able to go out.

Outside
it was nice.

But he was all alone,
the stars had not
come back.

Fortunately,
new people
greeted him;
half-suns
half-stars.
They taught him
how to live again
in full daylight.

Now, he knows
he is a star.

And he shines.